If I Were Your Mother

Margaret Park Bridges

Illustrated by Kady MacDonald Denton

Morrow Junior Books

NEW YORK

To Holly and Emma, for making everything worthwhile.

—M. P. B.

For D.L.L.D.

—K.M.D.

Watercolors were used for the full-color illustrations.
The text type is 15-point Opti Adrift.

Published by Morrow Junior Books
a division of William Morrow and Company, Inc.
1350 Avenue of the Americas, New York, NY 10019
www.williammorrow.com

Printed in Singapore at Tien Wah Press.

1 3 5 7 9 10 8 6 4 2

Library of Congress Cataloging-in-Publication Data
Bridges, Margaret Park.
If I were your mother / Margaret Park Bridges; illustrated by Kady MacDonald Denton.
p. cm.
Summary: A girl tells her mother all the special things she would
do for her if their positions were reversed and she was the mother.
ISBN 0-688-15190-6 (trade)—ISBN 0-688-15191-4 (library)
[1. Mother and child—Fiction.] I. Denton, Kady MacDonald, ill. II. Title.
PZ7.B76191h 1999 [E]—dc21 98-24132 CIP AC

Mommy, do you ever wish you were a little girl again?

Sometimes, honey.

Why, Mommy?

Sometimes I miss sitting in my mother's lap
and letting her take care of ME.

I could take care of you, Mommy.

You, my love?

Yes. I could pretend I was your mother and you were my little girl.

Well, if you were my mother, what would you do?

If I were your mother, I'd give you a big canopy bed
and bring you breakfast on a silver tray.

With a silver bell to call you when I was done?

No, because I'd stay and keep you company.

If I were your mother, I'd let you go to school in my silky red party dress.

And high heels?

Even on gym day!

If I were your mother, I wouldn't get mad if you
left the door open and the neighbor's dog ran inside.

Even if she left muddy paw prints all over the carpet?

Even if.

If I were your mother, I'd take you to work and let you dance on my desk.

And spin me around in your chair?

Till you were all dizzy from going round and round!

If I were your mother, I would build
a giant tree house for you and your friends.

With an elevator?

Yes—and a firefighter's pole to slide down.

If I were your mother, I would let you curl my hair
and make up my face and paint my fingernails.

So you could look beautiful?

So I could look SILLY!

If I were your mother,
I'd let you jump from the sofa to the armchair.

And lay the cushions across the floor like stepping stones?

Yes, so you could cross the room without touching the floor.

If I were your mother, I would give you a bath with goldfish.

What if they splashed water all over the floor?

Then they'd have to clean it up.

If I were your mother, I'd wrap you in a big, thick towel
after your bath to keep you warm and cozy.

Like a cocoon?

Yes—and then you'd fly like a butterfly into your pajamas.

If I were your mother, I would pretend to be
a monster coming to get you under the covers.

You mean a MOMster?

Yes! But I wouldn't scare you—just tickle.

If I were your mother,

I'd let you sleep in Granny's soft, furry coat.

Inside out?

With your legs in the sleeves.

If I were your mother, I'd kiss your forehead every night
so you'd have sweet dreams.

What would I dream?

You'd dream the stars were sprinkles on a chocolate ice cream sky—and you'd eat it all up!

You could always tell me your dreams...

And if I were your mother, I would always listen to you, no matter what you said.

Even if I whispered?

Even if you didn't use any words at all. I would always listen.

Well, you certainly would
be a good mother, my love.

But, Mommy?

Yes?

Right now, can you be MY mother again and just hold me in your lap?

Of course, my love. Always.